THE STORY OF GOD'S GREAT PLAN

# MARY, DID YOU KNOW?

ILLUSTRATIONS BY PHIL BOATWRIGHT

# MARK LOWRY

WATERBROOK
PRESS

COLORADO SPRINGS

MARY, DID YOU KNOW?

PUBLISHED BY WATERBROOK PRESS

5446 North Academy Boulevard, Suite 200

Colorado Springs, Colorado 80918

*A division of Random House, Inc.*

Scripture quotations are adapted from several translations.

ISBN 1-57856-179-5

Printed in the United States of America

1998

10 9 8 7 6 5 4

# A MOTHER'S MOMENTS

YOU MAY THINK Mark Lowry's mother needs a crown in glory just for being his mother. At least after she raised him she went back to college and got a *cum laude* graduate degree in psychology, and she says that after what Mark taught her, school was a breeze!

I just know that I for one am glad that Beverly Lowry gave birth and gave time to a son called Mark. He is a gift to my life, and — as funny as he is — one of the most serious and dearest people I know.

I suppose if Mark's mother had known what she was getting into when she first held that little boy in her arms, she might have had second thoughts. But then if any of our mothers had known all that lay ahead, they might have backed out of the deal.

As a mother, I know I am glad I didn't know it all. But now as I look at my son, I am, more than anything, thankful. Thankful that God chose me to be his mother. Thankful for the whole experience we have walked through together to bring us to this moment.

Thankful that no matter what the future holds, God chose the experience of "my son" to make me what I am becoming.

Mary, too, more than any mother in history, was shaped by her son...literally! She knew less, yet knew more than any mother who ever lived, about what she was getting herself into. From the vantage point of Golgotha, however, she must have been overwhelmed at how little she had known that night when an angel blew into her life the Breath of Life.

But — as with all mothering — the hardest, most painful moments are eclipsed by the glory of watching your child resurrected into something more amazing than you could have ever imagined. And every mother knows that the most amazing gift of all is finding that only when she said "goodbye" to her son did she hear the words and know the reality: "Lo, I am with you always, even unto the end of the world."

Mary, did you know...?

GLORIA GAITHER

# A SONG IS BORN

IT STARTED WITH a bunch of questions. Questions I'd been pondering since I was a kid. They were sparked by a comment I heard my mother make many years ago: "If anyone knew Jesus was virgin-born — *Mary* knew. And no one could take that away from her."

Mary knew. And as Jesus grew up and the Father revealed so many things to Him — could He have used Mary to do some of the revealing?

I think so. Can you imagine the bedtime stories Mary must've told Jesus? Stories of stars, stables, and singing angels. Stories of shepherds and wise men from afar. Stories of prophets and priests and promises.

Can you imagine? She had been chosen to deliver God into the world. To nurse Him. To love Him. To protect Him. And, like every mother, to teach Him. She taught God how to walk. She taught Him how to talk. She changed God's diapers. She was chosen by God to raise the Son of God. And she watched Jesus grow in favor with God and man.

But how much did she know? Did she know about Gethsemane? Did she know about the cross? Did she know there would be a resurrection?

There was no one she could turn to for advice. She couldn't go to her mother and ask, "Mom, what was it like when you had your first virgin-born son?" No one had ever been down that road before. This was a first...and a last.

But what was it like raising God's Son? Did He ever skin His knees? Did He ever wrestle with His little brothers? What subject in school was His best? Did He ever take a fish and feed the neighborhood? Did Mary ever see Him embarrassed? Did she ever have to make Him get a haircut? Did He have a hero? Did He have a girlfriend? Was He a tenor or a bass? Did He laugh a lot? Was He ever moody? Did He ever have a weight problem? Was He ever homesick?

I couldn't get all these questions in the song. And I'll never really have the answers until I get to heaven and ask Mary for myself. Many of these questions probably don't deserve an answer anyway. But I picked a few of my favorites and put them down on paper.

I kept this lyric in my briefcase for several years, trying to get a composer to put music to it. One weekend, while traveling on the Gaithers' bus, I handed it to Buddy Greene and asked if he would give it a try.

He called me the following Monday and sang "Mary, Did You Know?" to me over the phone.

I liked it.

MARK LOWRY

# Mary...

did you know

that your

## baby boy...

will one day

**walk** on water?

*Very late in the night,*
*Jesus went out to His disciples*
*by walking on the sea…*
*(Matthew 14:25)*

# Mary,

did you know

that your baby boy

## will save

our sons and daughters?

*Jesus said,*
*"I have come... to save the world."*
*(John 12:47)*

Did you **know**

that your baby boy

has come to

make **you new?**

The child that you've

delivered will soon

**deliver you.**

*Anyone who belongs to Jesus Christ*
*is a new person. Old things are gone,*
*and everything is new!*
*(2 Corinthians 5:17)*

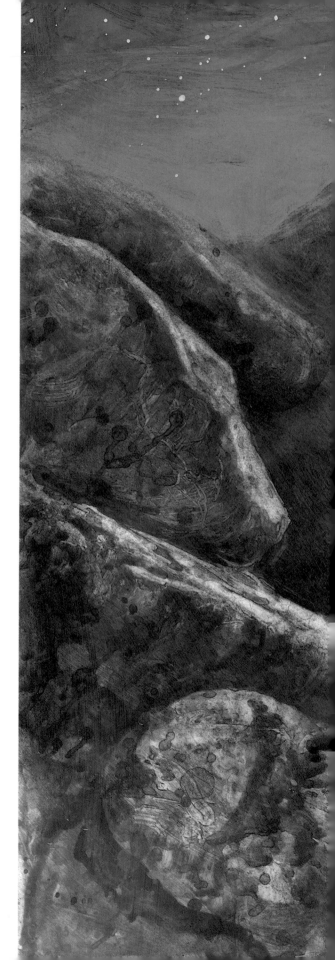

# Mary,

### did you know

## that your baby boy will

# give sight

### to a blind man?

*"Lord, let me see!" the blind man said.*
*Jesus answered, "Look then, and see—*
*your faith has healed you!"*
*(Luke 18:41-42)*

15

Mary, did you

know that your

baby boy will

## calm a storm

with His hand?

*Jesus stood up*
*and ordered the wind and the waves to stop;*
*suddenly everything was perfectly still!*
*(Matthew 8:26)*

16

Did you know

that your

baby boy

has walked where

angels trod?

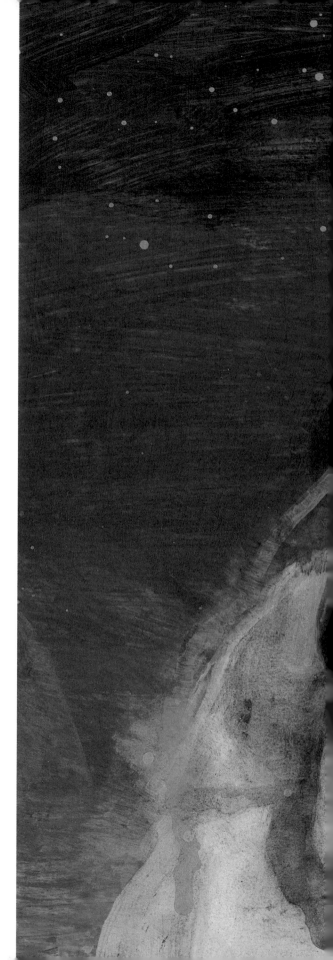

When **you kiss**

your little baby

you've kissed the

**face of God.**

The blind will **see**...

The deaf will **hear**...

The dead will live again.

The lame will **leap**...

The dumb will speak

the praises of

the **Lamb!**

*Jesus went around doing good*
*and healing all who were hurt by the devil,*
*because God was with Him.*
*(Acts 10:38)*

# Mary,

### did you know

### that your baby boy

## is Lord

### of all creation?

*God's Son is before everything,*
*and through Him everything holds together.*
*(Colossians 1:17)*

Mary,

did you **know**

that your baby boy

will one day rule

## the nations?

*The angel said to Mary,*
*"...You are to call Him Jesus...*
*He will be great...*
*and His kingdom will never end."*
*(Luke 1:30-33)*

Did you know

that your **baby** boy

is heaven's

**perfect** Lamb?

*"Look!*
*Here is the Lamb of God!"*
*(John 1:29)*

This sleeping
**child**
you're holding

is the Great

# I Am.

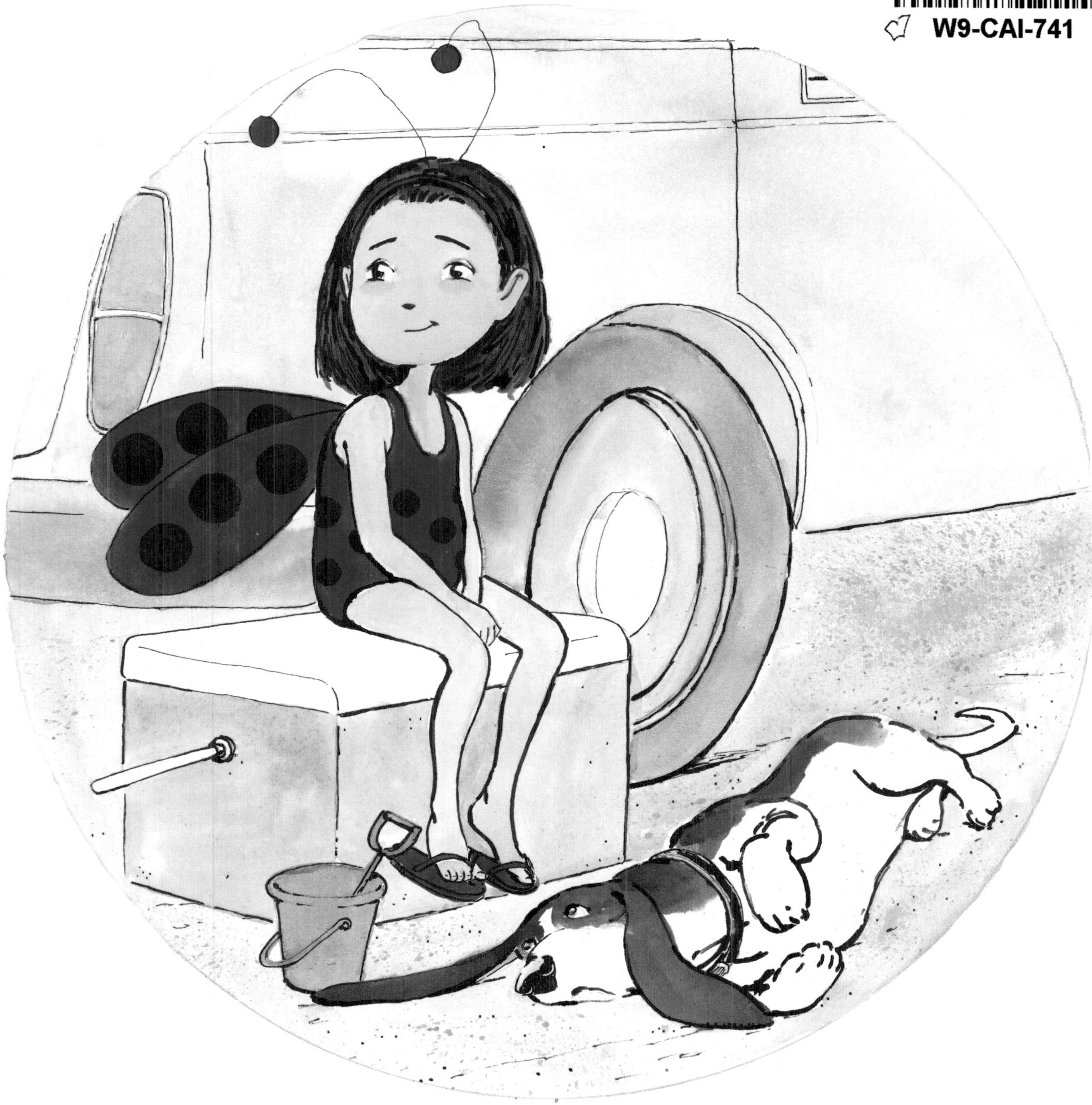

# Ladybug Girl at the Beach

by David Soman and Jacky Davis

SCHOLASTIC INC.

New York Toronto London Auckland
Sydney Mexico City New Delhi Hong Kong

To Joanne McParland, beach lover and midwife

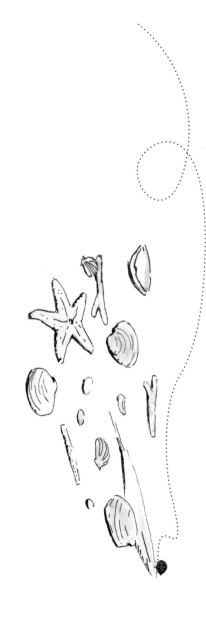

ISBN 978-0-545-45166-6

12 11 10 9 8 7 6 5 4 3 2 1          12 13 14 15 16 17/0

Printed in the U.S.A.          87

This edition first printing, January 2012

Designed by Teresa Dikun and Jasmin Rubero
Text set in Aunt Mildred

"We're finally here!" declares Lulu as she jumps out of the car and spreads her wings.

"I love the beach!" says Lulu.

"You've never even been to the beach before," replies her big brother.

"But I already know that I **love it**," she says. "And I can't wait to go swimming in the waves!"

The sand feels warm under her feet as Lulu and Bingo lead the family to a good spot to spread their blanket.

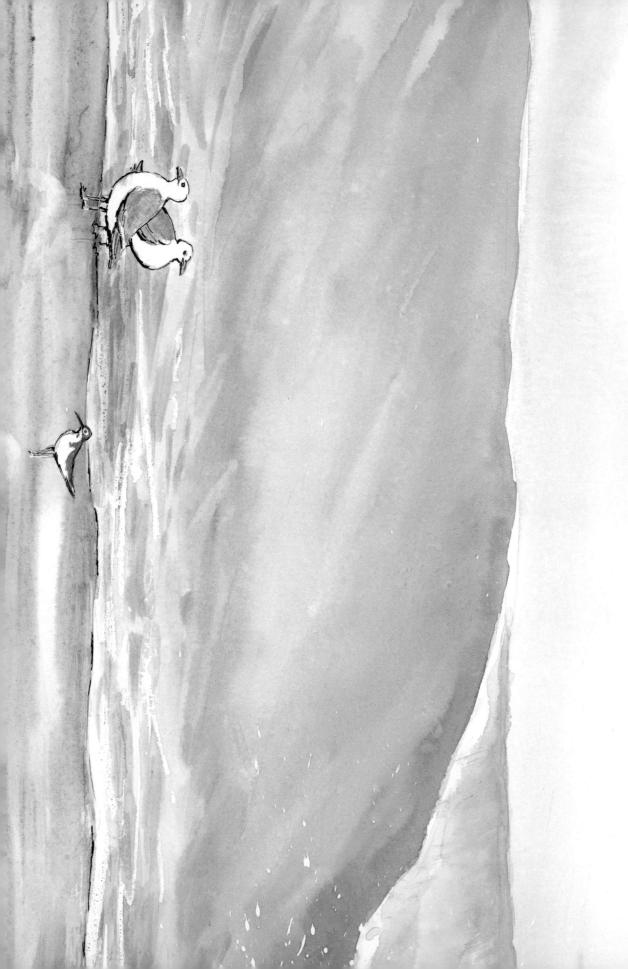

Lulu runs to the edge of the water.

The ocean goes on and on, and makes huge roaring sounds.

She had no idea it was going to be so big and noisy.

She takes a few steps backward. Bingo barks at the waves.

"Are you going in?" her brother yells, running
past her and splashing into the water.

"I don't think so," she says.

"Um . . . I really came here to build sand castles."

Lulu retreats to the beach blanket to find
her trusty pail and shovel.

She builds a giant sand castle, and uses little sticks for people. The King and the Queen are very happy here, she thinks. Bingo digs a moat to keep them extra safe.

Lulu walks over and sits down next to her mama. She looks out at the ocean, which is glittering with light. She thinks it looks pretty from far away.

"Do you want to go in the water?" asks Mama.

"No," Lulu says, "I want to fly the kite now."

Soon the kite is darting back and forth ir the wind, but Lulu holds on tight.

After the wind dies down, it feels really hot.
Lulu glances at the ocean.
She thinks the water would be cool,
but the waves still look much too big.

This is a good time to remind her parents about ice cream.

Lulu lists all her top eleven favorite flavors:

"Chocolate Marshmallow, **Cherry Vanilla,** Pistachio,

**Butter Pecan,** Peppermint Bon Bon,

Peanut Butter Chip,

**Raspberry Swirl,**

**Peach Pie,**

Almond Fudge,

Royal Banana Surprise,

and . . .

Vanilla."

At the ice cream stand Lulu can't just choose one.

"This is a day for a double scoop," her mama says.

Sometimes mamas can be very right.

"Come on, Bingo," says Lulu after she finishes her ice cream. "Let's take a walk down the beach!"

They find a long piece of driftwood. Lulu writes loopy L's in the sand, and draws pictures of Bingo. He's the perfect subject, and stays really still.

It is very hot. Lulu looks at the ocean.

Other kids are splashing and jumping in the waves.

She walks down to the edge of the water.

"Should we get our feet wet, Bingo?" she asks.

She thinks it would be okay to go into the ocean just a little bit.

Suddenly a wave crashes into her legs and nearly knocks her over.

Just as she gets her balance the whirling water races back and tries to pull her in. Her feet get buried in the sand up to her ankles.

"Are you okay, Bingo?" Lulu asks.

She looks around to see if anyone noticed
that they were almost carried away,
but everyone is playing just as they were before.

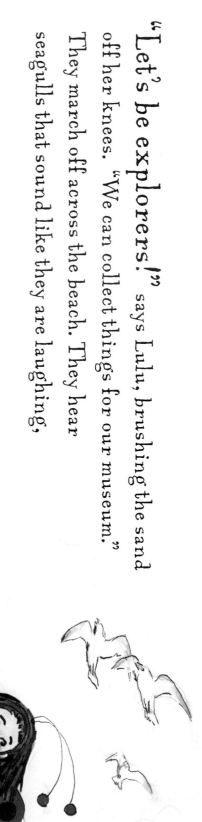

"Let's be explorers!" says Lulu, brushing the sand off her knees. "We can collect things for our museum." They march off across the beach. They hear seagulls that sound like they are laughing,

discover little crabs that burrow into the sand,

and pick up slimy seaweed washed up on shore.

There are also lots of shells on the beach,
all different shapes and sizes.
She chooses the most special ones
and puts them into her pail.

"I know, Bingo! I bet if we dig, we could find a pirate treasure!" says Lulu. She digs, and digs, and digs. Finding treasure is hard work.

When Lulu feels the water splash against her,

she spins around. The tide has come in!

It is taking away her favorite pail!

She has to rescue it or it will be lost forever!

This is a job for Ladybug Girl!

"I'll save you!" she says, snapping up the pail.

When she looks down she realizes she is in the ocean.

She is actually **in** the ocean!

The water is past her knees, and she isn't afraid at all!

"Ladybug Girl isn't afraid of anything!"

For the rest of the long afternoon,

Ladybug Girl and Bingo splash in the water
and run on the beach daring the waves to catch them.

"You can't get me, waves. I'm Ladybug Girl!"

Ladybug Girl and Bingo play until

the bright blue sky turns pink.

They make footprints in the sand.

At least 14 miles of them, Ladybug Girl thinks.

Every time the ocean erases them, they make more.

Then it is time to go, and Ladybug Girl

trudges back across the still-warm sand.

Bingo follows slowly, dragging his ears.

Standing at the top of the dunes,
Ladybug Girl waits for her brother.

"So, did you like your first time at the beach?" he asks.

"Yes," she answers.

"I told you, Ladybug Girl loves the beach!"